Octavius Nash Ogden

Halimah

a legend of the Tangipahoa

Octavius Nash Ogden

Halimah
a legend of the Tangipahoa

ISBN/EAN: 9783337391317

Printed in Europe, USA, Canada, Australia, Japan

Cover: Foto ©Andreas Hilbeck / pixelio.de

More available books at **www.hansebooks.com**

HALIMAH

A LEGEND OF THE TANGIPAHOA

O. N. OGDEN

NEW ORLEANS
1891

PRESS OF
L. GRAHAM & SON,
NEW ORLEANS,

PREFACE.

The subject presented to the public in this little volume was suggested to the author during a residence at Amite City, the beautiful suburban town lying almost upon the banks of the Tangipahoa River.

Remnants of the aboriginal Indian tribes linger there, preserving to a great extent, amid the march of civilization, the primitive manners and habits of their ancestry. The weird spirit of the past seems still to breathe about the flower-lit margins of the arrow-like silver streams that intersect this region.

Geographically, the scenes are principally comprised in what is commonly known as the Florida Parishes of Louisiana. The invasions of foreign adventurers are historical and there exists even now a tradition of mineral wealth concealed in the picturesque hills. The title name, Halimah, was obtained from a Choctaw Indian still living. The volume is given to the public rather with the hope that it may attract abler exertions to a rich province of romance, than with any expectation of applause.

THE INVOCATION

THE INVOCATION

———

Tell, whispering Spirit of these fair retreats,
As softly echo your sad tale repeats
Like tender murmuring of a streamlet near,
Whose faint low music dies upon the ear;
Tell, from the woodland seat and sylvan dell,
What sacred memories in thy bosom dwell!
Translate the mystery of the silent glades,
Revive the pale Past's image ere it fades,
Awake the mourning forest's primal race,
Repeople solitude with life and grace!

What time Tangipahoa from mountain source,
Swelled thro' these haunts with brimming crystal
*   course—*

13

Triumphant wound its channel to the lake,
Thro' crowned banks of tree, and vine and brake;
Spurning each barrier to its foaming wrath,
O'erleaping here, and cleaving there a path,
Till conquering hill, it broadens in the plain,
And pours with lucid flood in Pontchartrain.

What time the antlered monarch of the wood
Securely cooled his hot flank in the flood,
And panting, as he paused in shallow flow,
Received a shaft, winged by the mortal bow—
Reared high in air his proudly crested head,
As look reproachful from his glance is sped—
Then yields in death unto the ruthless tide,
Empurpled by his redly ebbing side.

What time when April freshly clad the plain,
The pompous turkey proudly led his train,

And spreads to earth his pinions, rustling fans,
And amorous, every tempting female scans;
He struts with sounding wings upon the hills,
And passion vainly swells in blushing gills.
Sudden the savage marksman's eager sight
Aims true the flashing arrow's fatal flight;
The feathery dart speeds on its cruel quest
And quivers now within the glossy breast—
Stretched on the heath the gallant cock expires.
His heart's blood quenching its own kindling
    fires.

Or say, where deeply tangling coverts pen
The bear and panther in their gloomy den,
How e'en within these terror-bristling shades,
In quest of sport, the savage foot invades;
Surprising in their dangerous solitudes
The grim co-partners of the primal woods.

Roused from retreats erstwhile to man unknown,
Hedged by a wilderness with briar upgrown,
The hardy forest sons, with eager face
And savage glee, all fearless, start the chase.
Breathless pursue the sullen, crafty prey,
Till tracked remorseless to his desperate bay;
There art, not strength, prevails at last to win,
And decks the victor with the reeking skin.

Say how, ere driven from his lonely boughs,
Soothed by the towering pine tree's windy soughs,
The bleak, bald eagle watched his quarry fly—
Then in pursuit wheeled thro' the yielding sky;
O'ertopped the forest's pride, and shrieking loud,
Burst like a thunderbolt athwart the cloud;
Still presses sun-ward with an unblenched sight
And grasped the victim in empyrean light.
Luckless the flight! a winged arrow flies,
The nerveless talons drop their bleeding prize;

The soaring monarch, dead and fallen now,
Is plucked to plume the Indian's warlike brow.

Tell how and whither, exiled far to roam,
The Pelican forsook her wonted home;
Yet not before a trail of noble mind
Was left a legacy to human kind.
So when the escutcheon of vainglorious State
Boasts proudly mottoes of the Just and Great,
The parent Bird appears with bosom wrung,
And breast transpierced to feed her famished
    young.

With themes like these thy murmurous voice is
    fraught,
If chance aright its echoes have been caught.
Ah! now, propitious touch the proffered chords,
Which fain would tremble to thy mystic words!

Soft! now, methinks, a kind consenting mood
Inclines the gentle Spirit of the Wood—
With touches light as dropping dews she flings
Her fairy fingers o'er the waking strings,
And, gently as the notes which Angels hear,
Floats her weird music on the ravished ear:

HALIMAH

HALIMAH

Seekst thou to know when once these solemn pines
Were reverent trimmed, as Nature's sacred shrines;
The almost voiceless Past that haunts these glades,
With ghostly cadences from sombre shades;
Wouldst music wake to its accustomed thrills,
That now is scarce an echo on the hills?
Or, wouldst the note of savage mirth or rage,
To equal shock the sense of this nice age?
Long since the crumbling altars perished lie,
Where smoked the victim grateful to the sky;
Long since is hushed the tuneful choir of trees
That gave full vocal tribute to the breeze.

When Nature's worship, with untutored prayer,
Rose in its rude petition on the air.
Art's temple. now reverberate with praise,
Has drowned the feebler music of those days;
But ah! not sweeter, truer worship rose
From pealing organ as its anthem flows,
Than from these nature-tuned exalting notes,
Poured from the forest's myriad warbling throats.
The vocal choir 's dissolved, but still the sprays
Seem trembling where the songsters poured their lays :
And even yet some straggling minstrels cling
To the loved bough above the gurgling spring.

Where Mandeville's white sands shine on the beach.
Far as embracing waves caressing reach,
And bear a tribute from the ocean cells
To deck the shore with white and sculptured shells ;
Still in the orange grove green o'er the lake,
The mock-birds yet their scented trysting make,

And high and amorous on the balmy air,
The rival songsters serenade the fair.

To strains of rapture oft the contest thrills,
And notes fantastic pour from mimic bills:
Demure, coquetting on some odorous tree,
The flattered female drinks the minstrelsy,
And long bewildered in her loving choice,
Selects the mate that charms the most with voice.
And undeserting still, the spotted thrush,
In some deep glen at evening's dreamy hush,
Mellifluent swells her yellow throat with song,
That floats in tender tone the vales among;
Like some fair mourner, who with sacred breath,
Chants low a funeral dirge at twilight's death.
Sad! that the march of man's empire, ere long
Will still the music of the forest's song;
For when at last the savage realm 's subdued,
He wrecks its minstrelsy and wins a solitude.

Too plain alas! the doom of this retreat,
Where long I've made my consecrated seat,
Nor envied proud Parnassus' vocal shades,
Content to loiter in these tranquil glades,
Lulled by the scarce caught murmur of the streams
That flow with rill-like melody of dreams.
Portentous echoes now from startled hill
The scream of locomotive fierce and shrill:
With trampling fury and with fiery speed,
His iron hoof beats down the flowery mead;
With scorching breath from nostril smoking high,
The thunderous monster madly rushes by,
As if on Vulcan's anvil, frame and wheel,
And nerve and sinew, had been forged of steel.
The wondering savage and the quivering brute,
Gaze on the prodigy, with fear struck mute:
Well they foresee usurping Art's design,
Their realm confiscate and their ended line—
For now see commerce other handmaids charge
The newly conquered province to enlarge.

The haughty steamer climbs Tchefuncta's tide,
And nobly plows a foaming pathway wide;
And spurns the fragile fleet with billowy force,
That seeks to stay it on its conquering course.
The natives watch her agents thread the pines
And hang the sky with long electric lines,
Which hum o'erhead the mystic message sent,
To traverse in a flash the continent.
Startled—attend articulate whispers borne
Across these wires breathed by telephone.
As if the nimble sprites that people space
Were winged by vivid lightning for the race.

Ah! these are signs which fatal truths convey—
The Choctaw's empire 's doomed to pass away.
Farewell the silence of his wide domain!
Farewell unchallenged haunt of hill and plain!
The wigwam peace, the log-piled fireside,
Where proud at eve was dressed the family pride;

Where the swarth brow of the tall red-skin chief
Found soothing solace when it ached with grief;
Where meekly solemn sat with matron grace
The pensive squaw won from the hostile race—
Raped from the hut of some grim Chickasaw
What time the woods rang with the savage war,
And borne reluctant over hill and wave,
To cheer the wigwam of the Choctaw brave;
Like Sabine maid, borne off a Roman wife,
The tender nuptials bound in sanguine strife—
Her yielding fancy, soothed its vain alarms,
Forgets lost kindred in her warrior's arms.

About the skin-dressed hearth at close of day
The dusky forest children romp and play;
Hang listening, as some rude but graphic tongue
Recounts the deeds of wars as yet unsung;
And as the tragic doom of tribes is told,
The blood-red epic feeds the martial soul.

But in the group which breathless there attend
Each thrilling story to its direful end,
With brown cheek blanching and with heart - pulse
      wild,
Shrinks tremulous the wigwam's maiden child.
Her throbbing bosom and the tear that stole
Adown her cheek bespeak the tender soul—
Proclaim that e'en where savage nature sways,
Lost and perverted from the purer days,
High virtues still the savage hut adorn
And Mercy there survives when other gems are gone.

The breath of twenty springs with ripening warm
Matured Halimah's tall but rounded form,
And beauty clung about her like the dower
Of her dark woodland home's deep blushing
      flower—
The red Camelia—whose pure scentless face
Still native blooms in all unrivaled grace.

Or had she in consenting nuptials signed
When Tchappapela's brave sued for a bride.   *   *   *

Her dark, luxuriant tresses wildly rolled
As if their flow some frolic Grace controlled,
And wanton round her nut-brown neck, and chased
By amorous zephyrs, sport about her waist.
The gentle orbs tho' now with tears bedewed,
Know how to sparkle in the gayer mood:
Ne'er more brightly soft or softly bright the doe,
Gazelle - eyed, darts her glances shy and low,
Than as the trains of joyous fancy wake,
Her subtle spirits thro' these windows break:
Romp in her eye and dimple in her cheek,
And from her luscious lips in laughter speak,
As tho' their accents were decreed above
To be the tuneful oracles of Love.

Well might Chinchuba's wigwam, richly dressed
And hospitably bright, attract the guest;
And well might lusty braves of hill and plain
At old Chinchuba's door their mustangs rein.

The viewless couriers that speed the fame
Of beauty's marvels love to breathe her name.
Where soft Pearl River chants to echoing sound,
And blue Biloxi's Bay is girt around
With high and fragrant banks, the rumor 's borne,
Till beating hearts are trembling to its tone.
Yet not o'er painted, when with partial praise
Each charm it softly whispers, and portrays
The magic of the form's voluptuous grace,—
The perfume breathing from her rose - lit face,—
The fragrance of the ripely swelling breast,
As if sweet-olive there had late been pressed.
And ah! still more to nobly feed the flame,
Her changing spirits as they went and came,
Now tender as the calm of breathless seas,
And rippling now like wavelets in a breeze.

*With prelude thus the Spirit paused to bind
A straggling tress that wantoned with the wind,*

And stilled the fluttering drapery of her limbs
Whose breezy toilet some fond wood nymph trims.
And like the bird that on some sheltered spray
Eyes o'er and smoothes her feathery array,
She calms her scattered robes to graceful rest,
And breathing Jessamine fastens in her breast.

Ah! Mortal, sure your rapt expression well
Denotes the force of young Halimah's spell.
Her spirit charms us still from vacant bowers
Like lingering odors of the vanished flowers.

But no! these chords should sound with happier
      themes
To please the fancy of your Forest Dreams.
Seek not to rend the misty veil of years
Now closely drawn upon her smiles and tears;
Yea, let fond memory, which the scene surveys,
Recall her only in the halcyon days—

Ere the accursed hour the stranger came
To make the sobbing wave bewail her name.

To cause her eye to smile, her cheek to bloom,
I fain must wake her from her lucent tomb,
Where, hidden in the watery depths, her soul
Seems babbling still to every pebbly shoal.
Happy indeed had been her blameless life,
'Mid changing seasons, as some young buck's wife;
Oh! had she listened when with ardent voice
Abita's stalwart youth bade her rejoice;
Or had she in consenting nuptials sighed
When Tchappapela's brave sued for a bride;
Or faithful had she kept the soft breathed vow
Her young lips uttered neath the beechen bow,
Ere parting sped Natalbany's tall lover,
While watching birds approving sang above her.
Blessed, and blessing still in wonted wild,
She long had lived the petted forest child.

And still maturing into matron charm
Had nursed young heroes in the rude wigwam,
Till in the round mausoleum high and green
Interred with all her tribe she left the scene.
Yes, crowned her life had been with every joy
Had not the Spaniard entered to destroy.

THE VOYAGE

THE VOYAGE

The polished Spaniard who forsook his land
To seek adventure on a foreign strand—
Who, fired with thirst of Gold, all danger braves,
And trusts his bounding vessel to the waves.
The brazen prow drives thro' Atlantic gate,
Leaps in the Gulf with filling sails elate :
Sails like the white gull, devious in its course,
When on its wings a black squall spends its force—
Tops foaming seas and spurns the wave with scorn,
Till Ocean pinions flutter in Lake Borgne.

Now, whitening beach in lengthening line appears,
Where eastward shine the shell-piled Chandeleurs;
Then hastening past the brightly shining bays,
She glances thro' the narrow Rigolets,
And clearing, anchors in a watery plain,
As a proud conqueror of a new domain.

High sounds the song triumphal, as it fills
The air with echoes from saluted hills:
High flows the bumper, as the sylvan view
Awakes new transports in the pirate crew.
The night, to slumber given, dawns with the light
That brings a rising continent to sight.
How welcome to their eyes these coasts unfold,
As if the kindly yielding realms of Gold:
How fine to watch the tumbling porpoise play,
And greedy sharks voracious cut their way:
The leaping tarpon sun his silver sides,
The finny shoals that vex the foaming tides:

The crab float in his rugged emerald shell,
And sidelong dart, with claw so blue and fell;
The speckled trout spring high to catch the fly,
And spotted red-fish flashing swiftly by.
And then, the rapturous vision which expands
All gently on the soft defining lands.
And oh! the thrill with which the sense is whirled,
As in the growing landscape they salute a world.

In the swarth ranks of the sun - beaten crew
The pale commander towered — his eye of blue
All strangely mingling a serener light,
With darker rays that flash so fiercely bright.
As foremost at the poop erect he stands,
He looked the uncrowned king of the new lands.
In the firm face, so tranquil yet so bold,
Lit up by passion, which the will controlled,
There shone the daring soul on conquest bent,
That seeks a trophy in a continent.

The Spurning Bows from the port
A run out from the sea . . . .

And loudly as the wild huzzas now ring
They bless the sceptre of their Pirate King;
And while the brimming cup high flows, the song
Rolls echoing the sounding shores along.

Let weak and timid pinions still
    Their feeble flight restrain,
Content to skim the lowly hill,
    Or scour the stretching plain.

The eagle soars where storm - clouds break,
    And revels in the roar;
Let little boats, ambitious, make
    A cruise about the shore.

The splashing billows' foam shall burst
    Across our fearless prow—
In unplowed seas we'll be the first
    To raise a dauntless brow.

Let others track illusive path
  That wrecks with rock and reef,
We'll follow thro' the tempests' wrath
  Our brave intrepid chief.

Who points our course unerring straight,
  Where leads his lucky star,
Triumphant to the golden gate
  Of glittering Florida.

Then quick dispersing, when again they toast
The lucky Genius of the nearing coast.
The snowy tackle, with the east wind swelled,
Obeys the helm that now is westward held.

As evening shadows darken to their eyes
The expected shore, that gray before them lies,
Sudden, as they steer, while scarce a furlong's reach
Divides the bark from the advancing beach.

The sky 's o'ercast—the laboring vessel rocks
With gusty touches of the equinox;
And frequent from the darkly clouded north
The vivid lightning flames and flashes forth.
No flood pours from the heavy mantling cloud,
No breaking thunders mutter deep or loud,
But ever quick and momently the light
Gives panoramic glimpses brief and bright—
Yet snatched by darkness ere the eye can trace
The mystic features of fair nature's face.
Deciphered faintly, some titanic oak
Seemed an immortal sentinel, that spoke
A challenge to the haughty stranger band
That fain would raise a standard on the land;
Caught thro' the wide and flashing lightning's play,
Tall ghostly pines stretch out in dim array;
By hasty glimpse revealed magnolias high
In leafy grandeur wave upon the sky.
Anon, the breathless vault is black again,
And shyly peeping rise the starry train;

Their mellow sparkle steeped in evening dews
Seems a soft slumbrous spirit to diffuse.
So sweetly come these handmaids of the moon,
Who rises from her eastern chamber soon,
To reign with crescent sceptre in these courts,
In silence only broke by wakeful mockbird notes.

Who has not that has rocked upon the main
In distant voyage sighed for land again!
Grand is the ocean when its billows bright
Burst round the keel in phosphorescent light,
And like the lofty tone of some high psalm
Its echoing roar remembered in the calm,
Its terror gone; but the deep cadence yet
Rings with a voice we never can forget.
And beautiful the deep blue stretch of seas,
As, all unbroken by the breath of breeze,
It spreads afar a stainless mirror, given
For Angel faces that look down from Heaven.

But yet how sweet at last the smiling shore
With welcome's greeting as the journey's o'er!
When from the waves gradually clear,
The plain and lofty hill approach more near,
And as there steals fresh o'er the briny floods,
The incense of the flowery breathing woods.

Now for the night, like sea bird on the deep,
The bark reposes as the billows sleep;
The sail is furled, and whitely gleaming by.
Rushes the crested wave in lullaby.
The halyards coiled, and bare beneath the stars,
Like ghostly skeletons, uprise the spars,
As first significant with lofty sign
That here the conquering Cross shall shortly shine.
Yet hark! shrill sounding o'er the startled beach,
With baleful omen rings an owlet's screech;
As if a warning, burdened with distress
Were shrieking poured by some mad prophetess.

Unswung, the hammock is forgotten now,
And sleepless crowd the crew around the prow,
And thro' the breathless night in ceaseless watch
Eyes strain day's first revealing beams to catch.
So anchored high before the silent fort,
At morn to echo with the dread report.
The watching seamen thro' the darkness strain
To catch the rampart bristling o'er the main;
Yet o'er exultant hearts some shadows creep
To think what graves may yawn within the deep.
So mingling now with the transporting play
Of Fancy, dreaming at the break of day,
Foreboding fears will rise in stoutest heart
As phantom horrors from the mists upstart;
Or from untrodden shores a savage yell
Seems from the deepening glooms to sound a knell.

Yet when the day all grandly lights the scene,
High courage stirs the heart of bold marine;

And now majestic in the sun's first beams
The conquered coast in tranquil beauty gleams.
Like wearied Pilgrim after ocean's shock,
Gazing with rapture on gray Plymouth Rock,
Which shines inviting as his wanderings cease,
A stony stairway to a World of Peace,
They hail a landscape smiling on the shore,
All safe sequestered from the ocean's roar.
The crescent beach half circles in a bay,
In whose soft fold the glancing mullet play:
And myriad sardine shoal here refuge make
When preying monsters chase them thro' the lake:
All brightly gleams with glittering sands the beach,
And far its softly curving margins reach.
Oh! who that now the placid scene glanced o'er
Would tell it ere had known the tempest's roar?
And but for yon high pine despoiled and dead,
That solitary rears its branchless head,
Would deem the raging tempest ever smote
Secluded shore so tranquil and remote?

Long silent fed the rapt sense upon
Each charm expanding in the climbing sun;
At last instinctive, swelling from the throng,
Saluting rolls the pirates' lofty song:

Hail Freedom's wild but welcome strand
    That smiles upon the sea,
Wave long triumphant o'er the land
    The banner of the free!

Here let not Persecution tread
    Or Despot voice resound,
Where Independence wins the bread
    Of Plenty's fertile ground.

What tho' repeating gales still bear
    Upon the tell-tale breeze,
Our country's curses that declare
    Us pirates of the seas.

What 's banishment from Tyrant's ports,
　　Where Vice triumphant sways?
What 's exile from immoral courts,
　　Where Pride is wreathed with bays?

Here interpose long ocean miles,
　　Here dies pursuing blast,
And kindly Nature cheering smiles
　　Forgiving o'er the past.

Then welcome to the exile's heart
　　The free, inviting plain,
Where all his gloomy fears depart
　　And Hope springs fresh again.

Scarce die the echoes on the placid shores
When old Pedrillo from the flagon pours
Another bumper, and, with waving glass,
Thus drinks farewell to Spain's forgotten lass:

To a forsaken bower which now bewails
The fleeting lover and the cruel sails.   *   *   *

Let 's pledge brave boys to brighter eyes
    That soon will greet us here.
And drink to lips whose sweeter sighs
    Will wanton with the ear.

False Madrid maids we 'll then forget,
    When newer loves are kind,
And ere a dozen suns have set
    Will each a mistress find.

Loud rings the laugh, but o'er the chieftain's brow
A shadow darkened. Calm, serene till now,
A chord is touched, which trembles truly yet
To some fond thought the mind can ne'er forget.
A voice entreating seems to fondly plead,
And back his truant heart to gently lead
To a forsaken bower which now bewails
The fleeting lover and the cruel sails.
But soon the clouding shadow is dispelled,
And quick the rising sorrow now is quelled,

While stern and high rings out the loud command,
And rapidly the lowering boat is manned.
"To shore, to shore." The strong oars make replies
With sweeping strokes, and o'er the water flies
The boat like arrow, till a steering hand
Secures her safely on the yielding sand.
With Hope delirious their elastic feet
Invade the realm of Promise fair and sweet,
Nor marked the savage pause ere fatal springs
The envenomed shaft to try its deadly wings.
And now from ambush they advance, until
A challenge sounds in accent strangely shrill;
But quick, instinctive gesture finds a sign
To testify the strangers' friendly mind.
And soon the cautious Indians closer draw,
Nor longer menace with the show of war.
To kindlier mood all-winning tact soon charms,
And mutual now are banished all alarms;
Inspiring flasks impart a genial flow
And Spanish wine transforms the savage foe.

They watch the bark expand with tackle brave
And rock majestic on the swelling wave:
And still with signal eloquent they ask,
Whence flows the Spirit of the magic flask.

ARÇOLA

ARCOLA

※

Here restful weeks in converse kind are passed,
And Choctaw idiom is acquired at last:
But soon fond dreams of Gold their fancies thrill
As Legend whispers of a Mystic Hill,
Which rises softly, so the savage tells,
Where old Chinchuba hospitably dwells.
A lithe consenting brave assists their plans,
And offers guidance to the higher lands—

The swiftest yawl is launched, and gaily now
In Tangipahoa it points a gilded prow.

The rising orb of day in glory breaks
When high in bow Alvarez station takes;
And brightly towering o'er the wave there shone
A shell bank, reared as if for Naiad's throne —
There thro' the centuries it defies the tides
That break upon its slant and snowy sides;
A high memorial piled by savage hand
When Famine gaunt once walked the stricken land;
When parching skies refused the fruitful rain,
And earth's increase long failed on hill and plain.
There crowding from the desolated hills,
The famished horde the winding beach now fills,
And ocean kindly yields what earth denies,
And bountiful a store of fish provides.
The plundered clam and rifled oyster shell
To feed the tribes in heaping banks now swell,

Till long repeating toils have piled them steep
In pyramid of shell above the deep.

The active guide now deftly plies his oar,
And speeds the yawl from the receding shore :
Wide first the inlet mouth appears a bay,
Descried all dimly in the early day.
Hemmed in with tall and rankly growing grass,
On either side there spreads a wide morass,
And as the dipping oars repeat their stroke
Some lazy grosbeck 's from his nest awoke ;
And fierce and shrill his signal warnings sound
To all the feathery tribe that there abound.
The startled wood - duck flies — the zig - zag snipe
Pours note alarming thro' its slender pipe ;
The noisy cormorants vociferous shout
In wild, distracting cries the marsh about ;
And light and graceful into motion wheel
To unsurpassed flight the blue-winged teal.

Swift thro' the marshy flat the yawl now speeds
To where the rising bank is clothed with reeds;
And gently narrowing, the gleaming flood
Shines now in silver pathway thro' the wood,
Where tower the cypress stalwarts of the swamp,
Arrayed and bearded in their mossy pomp;
Then softly swelling margins bound the tide,
And mantling vines rare, luscious clusters hide.

Anon, the murmuring stream winds 'neath a shade
Of densely bowering trees all darkly made;
And sportive in the beechen branches high
The leaping squirrels hold festivity.
The frightened raccoon clings to mossy fork,
And closely hugs the black oak's sheltering bark;
And in yon covert, gleaming like a lance,
The panther darts his cold and deadly glance;
And sluggish in the deepest jungle's shade
The clumsy bear his awful bed has made.

Where tower the cypress stalwarts of the swamp
Arrayed and bearded in their mossy pomp. * * *

Near by, upstarting in affright the deer,
With doe and dappled fawn their crowns uprear:
And solemn sits as hooded monk in cowl
In his green hermitage the lonely owl —
The oracle and prophet of the wood,
Since here his ancient home primeval stood.

But still as narrowing its crystal tide,
High flow'ring banks compress on either side,
And sweet, within the woods, delaying blooms
Of forest flowers emit their faint perfumes ;
For autumn now has touched with fingers cold,
And Midas - like converts the green to gold.
Ripe, high and luscious, on the hanging vines
All purpling glow the juicy muscadines :
And blushing, as they tempt the hand to rape,
Wave on the air full clusters of the grape.
Thus softly is the vacant mind beguiled
In passing thro' the lone unconquered wild ;

But when the evening beams declining rest
On wood, and vale, in Autumn beauty dressed,
As still the oars compel to higher lands,
And softer prospect into view expands,
There subtly breathes from opening wood and shade
The spirit of a haunt where man his home has
    made.
When boldly thro' the wild, forbidding waste,
The hardy traveler a path has traced.
And long encountered in drear scene and rude
But sight of wilderness and sound of flood,
He gladly sees e'en savage hut arise.
And hears exultant even savage cries.
So now when long thro' ruder nature wending,
Till o'er the scene the graceful shades are bending,
How welcome is each sign—the golden field
Of corn, that promises rewarding yield—
The clearing forest and the very air.
Denoting man, tho' savage man, lives there.

And still how dearer is to each advance
All soft appearing to delight the glance.
The tokens sweet that delicate female taste
Refines with lovely hand the dreary waste;
For here are blending with the native bowers
Detected odors of exotic flowers.

The taste of Woman! Oh the magic hand,
That rules her realm as with a fairy wand!
O'er chaos waves and instant smiles a scene,
That rises up in charm to bless its Queen.
Oh! Woman, since you left Elysian bowers,
Thy faithful task has been to train the flowers,
As tho' a portion of lost Eden's doom,
Condemned thy hand to win again their bloom.

But now the eye descries, high and aloof,
Above the beech trees rise Chinchuba's roof,
On ridge that green and parallel extends,
And flanks the river as it northward wends;

And further east a hill's tall, shining crest,
Flames forth with dying glory of the west;
It softly rose in golden sunset sea,
Laving the border of Eternity
Where transient clouds seemed touched with sacred
        fire,
To glow with changing grace ere they expire.

The strong and patient guide moors fast the yawl
And sounds upon the air his signal call;
The stalwart brave decked in barbaric pride
Descends the slope and greets the Indian guide.
Few words and signs soon briefly recommend,
From Choctaw friends below, the ocean friend —
And quick extended is saluting hand,
That grasps the pale face welcome to the land.
Cordial now high, mutual glances range,
And greeting looks their lofty souls exchange.
Each, instant reads the signet courage gave
To character the brows of all the truly brave.

Their tall forms now retreating from the shore,
Loom in the glade before the opening door,
Which swings in rustic welcome high and wide,
And shows the cheerful blazing fire inside.
Fleet, nimble feet, on hastening errand fly
To do as bid by hospitality.

And dost thou here sweet lingering human grace
Still light the hearthstone of the darkened Race,
And shine amid the wood and touch to smile
The rugged features of the forest child?
Ah! yes: tho' here with no vain trimming clad
Thy smiling face beams radiantly glad;
For even here in this far savage land,
Behold the graceful ministry of thy hand!

But didst thou note the new and lovely glow,
Deep as the red which blushing doth bestow,
Which now adorning flushes, and now dies,
As on the stranger dwelt Halimah's eyes?

So tall, so fair! supernal graces seem
Responding to some shape revealed in dream.

The soul seems in mysterious depths to keep
Some slumbering memories waking in our sleep,
Impressions subtly graven of a past
Whose dim familiar features beam at last.
And oft our memories do seem to show
Fantastic images of a long ago,
And strangely, vaguely haunt us with a shore
Or scene or face we somewhere saw before.

Quick, kindly hands the frugal board prepare,
And hunger banquets on the homely fare,
Where juicy roast of venison and fish,
With forest fruits, are served in earthen dish.
The added luxury of the Spaniard's wine
Regales the company that hearty dine;
And as more chatty grows the fluent tongue
To eager ears the stranger's story 's sung:

"We come from where blue ocean waves high roll
Upon the coast of Spain, in search of Gold.
The shining ore which from these coasts we bring
Is worshipped there as proudest earthly king.
Crowns bend their jeweled diadems, and dim
The mitre's lustre doth appear to him;
Throned in the subject's and the prince's mind,
Such loyalty earth's potentates ne'er find;
For ne'er magician subtly charming till
He works the plastic spirit to his will,
Has yet with dark and necromantic art
So strongly to his spell bound fast the heart.
The sceptre of his sway gleams high and bold,
And earth bows now obsequious to Gold.
High o'er the wave which beats my native shore
A city rises far above its roar:
There every art and every science springs,
As prompting brain and hand, the potent metal rings.
Equipped and launched from busy sounding docks
Fleet navies breast the raging ocean's shocks,

We come from where the northern waves high roll
Upon the coast of Spain in search of Gold. * * *

To bear the tributary wealth of seas,
The sense to flatter and the mind to please.
On lofty heights high crownéd castles rise,
And gilded palace domes pierce thro' the skies.
Ransacked Arabia yields her rare perfume,
And gardens there are forced to tropic bloom;
Luxurious courts, ablaze with varied lights
And voluptuous with music's soft delights,
Their revels keep, touched into charm by Gold,
Which here unconscious these high hills may hold.

"Even genius servile flatters as he nods,
And poetry abjures her former gods,
Wreathes ivy chaplets on his glistering brow,
And breathes in lyric sweetness her soft vow.
Obedient pencils touch as he commands,
And sacred canvas lit by artist-hands,
Ideal glows with beauty freshly born
The high and frescoed chamber to adorn.

Sculpture's creative eye, at his behest,
Disturbs the marble's white and placid rest,
To chisel into life some laughing grace
That long lay sleeping in the stone's embrace.
Such power has Gold, whose secret shrines so bright
Are hid profoundly in rude nature's night.
When over boisterous sea man long has toiled
And still his step by rugged coast is foiled,
And every horror seems to hedge the prize
With dragon guard from his pursuing eyes;
Yet should the fairy realm but ope the door,
Forgotten are the pains endured before;
For honor high and proud distinction wait,
With wreath uplifted now to crown him great."

As thus he ended, old Chinchuba's face
Grew dark and serious, but resumed its grace,
As kind, but firmly ere they part for rest,
These ominous words are to his ear addressed:

" Right welcome, stranger, to our simple cheer,
Which scant but hearty we can offer here;
All freely tendered is our ample ground,
Where deer and bear and other game abound—
There freely wander as our savage child
In the unfettered freedom of the wild.
Make in our shelter your secure repose
Safe guarded here from beast, or human foes.
Still at our board the welcome place assume,
When quiet wigwam life thou wouldst resume.
But"—here all sternly glanced his kindling eye—
" One spot forego to enter, or you die.
By that strong tie which binds the host to guard
The guest from danger, and from harm to ward,
I warn you as you rove at freedom's will,
To dare not enter yonder sacred hill.
The grim and solemn Genius of our Race
Keeps holy vigil in that gloomy place,
And the intruding steps resents in wrath
That dares confront him in the circling path

He makes about the consecrated hill,
.Whose hollow, bones of perished tribes do fill."

The warning falls, and solemn now but kind,
He bids his startled guest compose his mind
With slumber, till the loudly sounding horn
Shall summon to the chase at early morn.
Now serious ere retiring, o'er the chance
Of that eventful eve he broods. The glance—
The voice of old Chinchuba echoing still
With fatal warning of the Mystic Hill
All fire his mind with anxious thought oppressed,
And vain he wooes deserting slumber's rest.

Now fancy would recall Halimah's grace,
Her flattering secret blushing in her face.
And then would muse on bower which still bewails,
The fleeting lover and the cruel sails.

But vain! resistless, conquering the will,
Unbidden thought arises of the Hill,

And shining there before his eye unrolled,
Lies gleaming treasure of the realm of gold.
His dauntless mind spurns superstitious tale,
Of vengeful demon guarding sacred pale:
And now as by strange fascination led,
He rises from his tossed, uneasy bed.

Without are starry heavens, serene and fair,
And scarce a murmur trembles in the air.
The moon to zenith risen all tranquil glides
And fatal to the Hill his footstep guides.
Unawed before, the solemn mien and air
Of old Chinchuba are remembered there;
And every chill and nipping touch of dew,
Seems all unwonted here to pierce him through.
But shall the valiant soul that braves a storm,
Shake at a wild, fantastical alarm,
That grim and marrowless ghost infests the place,
As guardian goblin of a buried race?

His halting spirit soon its tone resumes.
As soft and shadowy beam the scene illumes;
A nimble foot upon the rising mound
Is planted, yet all silent sleeps the ground.
"Sure," thought Alvarez, "idle tongues have lied,
That tell in place so sweet ghost would abide."

He presses firmly now with step more bold,
Till high, as if by man it had been rolled,
A huge and moss-grown rock appears to close
A cavern's mouth. But quick aside he throws
The stone obstruction; and to light his march
Within the dreary tunnel, bears a torch;
Wide and high and gloomy rise the walls,
As made for weird and ghostly goblin balls.
Still as he presses, sudden to his eye,
A spacious rocky chamber glitters high;
With gleaming arch and brightly shining side,
It seemed to flame in wondrous golden pride.

Alvarez spell-bound halts while fancy thickens
And pulse with thought unutterable quickens.
"Ah, here's the secret of the Mystic Hill,
And these the phantoms that its hollows fill.
All welcome terrors, come ye in such form,
The high exulting fancy so to warm,
With vision of a wealth more proudly grand,
Than loads the piled vaults of my rich land."
Still as he rapturous gazed at dazzling walls,
The gloomy passage echoes with footfalls;
And as the bodeful sounds more near advance,
With horror chilled he backward turns his glance.
And dimly lighted by the torch's glare,
He shuddering sees a figure groping there.
In vain he seeks the bounding pulse to still:
Behold! the Genius of the Mystic Hill!

Still groping onward, the tall figure now
Sudden reveals Chinchuba's stately brow:

Not beaming with the aspect late so kind,
But bristling fiercely with determined mind.
He sternly now surveys his startled guest,
With dark foreboding direful oppressed,
And slow and ominous his speech now falls,
As echoed by the golden, gleaming walls.

" I am the Genius of the Mystic Hill,
In solemn watch to guard its portals still!
When in my wigwam thou hast known this hand
To cordial welcome stranger to our land ;
By solemn warning I have sought to stay
Your feet when fatal they might careless stray.
The secret of this richly shining ore,
Must never pass beyond our happy shore.
To blast our native wilds with conquering bands,
To drive us from our far sequestered lands.
On high, Chinchuba's oath 's recorded long —
And stranger thou must join the *silent throng*."

Alvarez long his stalwart stature eyed,
Then half contemptuous tho' sad replied:
" I could not find a tomb more grandly bright,
Than here is hewn, lit with gold stalactite.
While ever cheering the cold sepulchre,
A costly splendor glitters nobly here:
Not in more pomp Egyptian king could rest,
With lofty pyramid above his breast,
Than here magnificence with golden cave
Has furnished forth a rich and princely grave.
And if the gathering fury of thy brow
Means peace has passed forever from it now,
And thou art bent thy bloody oath to keep,
As foe I raise a blade which else would sleep
Unstained in sheath; nor flashed but to defend
My honor, life, or interest of my friend."

Their weapons flash on high, and grim and tall
As shown by torchlight planted in the wall,

The Spaniard's tender unnerved mood is caught
And crashing cleaves the hatchet to his heart. * * *

Their faces gleam in wild unnatural palor,
Confronted in the deadly match of valor.
The graceful Spaniard aimed unerring blade;
The wily Indian artful parry made;
And equal long and furious raged the fight,
In such arena lit by torch's light.

And Spanish nerve and skill were sure to win,
When suddenly, above the battle's din,
A wild cry pierces thro' the ringing walls,
And prostrate at their feet Halimah falls.
Alvarez could not, gazing on her charm,
Direct his blade against the father's form;
But quick his foe, relentless, at a glance
Beheld advantage, and the lucky chance.
The Spaniard's tender, unnerved mood is caught,
And crashing cleaves the hatchet to his heart.
The firm face quivers and the senses fade:
He reels, embracing as he dies the maid.

And the mysterious, ghastly golden hill,
Its midnight secret dark is keeping still;
And unexplored is still the precious mine,
Whose golden chambers all unseen do shine;
And sadly murmuring the lucent wave
Sobs where Halimah rashly made her grave;
And still the Spanish bower all loud bewails
The fleeting lover's unreturning sails.

* * * *

Thus ends the Spirit her pathetic tale,
And vanishes in misty twilight's veil;
And ghostly face of savage seems to scowl;
From forest depth shrill shrieks the dismal owl.
And touching into dewy grief the sky
Rings far the Indian maiden's phrensied cry:

* * * *

Oh! cruel realm of shadows show
    Where thou dost hide my love!
Is he enchained in wave below,
    Or in blue deeps above?

Say envious reef with coral dyed,
    Dost thou fear pale eclipse,
And wouldst thou deepen thy red pride
    With his carnation lips?

Oh! bank of blue piled in the dome
    Of overarching sky,
Say, hast thou garnished angels' home
    With lustre of his eye?

Lend me, fair river sprite, thy shell,
    And light my way with smile,
And I will pierce each secret cell,
    And wake each silent aisle,

And win him back to where my bower
    Awaits with fragrant charms,
To lay him with a subtle power
    Revived within my arms.

www.ingramcontent.com/pod-product-compliance
Lightning Source LLC
Chambersburg PA
CBHW030005030726
47499CB00008B/2905